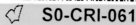
S0-CRI-061

The Three Bears

Retold by Rita Balducci
Illustrated by Jean Chandler

A GOLDEN BOOK • NEW YORK

Western Publishing Company, Inc., Racine, Wisconsin 53404

© 1991 Western Publishing Company, Inc. Illustrations © 1991 Jean Chandler. All rights reserved. Printed in the U.S.A. No part of this book may be reproduced or copied in any form without written permission from the publisher. All trademarks are the property of Western Publishing Company, Inc. Library of Congress Catalog Card Number: 90-85361 ISBN: 0-307-07065-4   MCMXCII

Once upon a time there was a little girl named Goldilocks. She liked to play at the edge of the woods near her house.

One day, as Goldilocks was making a chain of daisies, a delicious smell drifted through the trees.

"Oh, my!" she exclaimed. "That smells like yummy porridge!" And with that she jumped up and followed the smell right into the woods.

The delicious smell got stronger and stronger. Goldilocks heard her tummy rumble. "Why, I think I smell honey and cream, too!" she said. And deeper into the woods she went.

Goldilocks kept following the delicious
smell. It wasn't long before she found herself
walking up a path to a pretty little cottage.
"This must be where the wonderful smell is
coming from!" she said to herself. Then she
knocked on the door of the cottage.

There wasn't any answer. "I'm sure no one will mind if I just let myself in," Goldilocks thought as she turned the knob. The door creaked open, and she stepped in.

Inside, the good smell was even better, for there on the kitchen table were three bowls of porridge. And right beside them was a pitcher of sweet cream and a pot of clover honey.

By then, Goldilocks was so hungry that she forgot all about her manners. She ran to the table and began to eat the porridge in the biggest bowl.

"Ouch! This porridge is too hot!" she said. So she tried the porridge in the next bowl. "Oh, no! This porridge is too cold!" she said.

Then she decided to try the smallest bowl. "Yummy! This porridge is just right!" she cried. She poured on lots of honey and cream and ate and ate as fast as she could. But Goldilocks ate so much so fast that she began to have a tummy ache.

"Oh, dear," she said, looking at the mess she had made. She was too tired to clean up, so she went to the parlor to rest.

First she climbed into a big rocking chair.
She tried to close her eyes, but the chair was
not comfortable. "This chair is too hard!" she
said as she bounced off the chair.

Then she settled into a second rocking chair. It was soft and squeaked when it rocked. Goldilocks slid off the chair. "This chair is too soft," she said unhappily.

Next she saw a sweet little rocker, right beside the fireplace. "That's the chair for me!" she cried. She plopped down and—*CRASH*—the little chair broke into pieces.

"Oh, my!" said Goldilocks. "My tummy
hurts and I need to rest." So she climbed the
stairs and looked all around.

"I'll just lie down for a few minutes," she
said when she saw three cozy beds all in a row.

The first bed she climbed onto was broad
and high. Goldilocks lay down and then sat
up again. "This bed is too hard!" she
complained.

Then she tried the second bed. The soft feather pillow on the bed made her sneeze, and the mattress was lumpy. "This bed is too soft!" she said grumpily.

Then Goldilocks saw the little bed with a pretty red quilt on top. "That looks like a good bed for me!" she said happily. She lay down and fell fast asleep.

Just at that moment, the three bears who lived in the cottage came home.

"Someone's been eating my porridge!" shouted Papa.

"Someone's been eating *my* porridge!" cried Mama.

"Someone's been eating *my* porridge, too!" howled Baby Bear. "And they didn't leave any for me!"

Then they went into the parlor. "Someone's been sitting in my chair!" growled Papa.

"Someone's been sitting in *my* chair!" said Mama.

"Someone's been sitting in *my* chair!" cried Baby Bear. "I think it was an elephant!"

Then they followed Papa Bear as he raced
up the stairs.

"Who's been sleeping in my bed?" Papa bellowed.

"Who's been sleeping in *my* bed?" Mama cried.

"Someone's been sleeping in *my* bed, and she's still here!" shouted Baby Bear, pulling the covers off Goldilocks.

Goldilocks sat up. She looked at the three bears. Then, quick as a wink, she jumped up and flew down the stairs. Out of the cottage she ran.

Goldilocks ran back to her own safe home.
She never wandered into the woods again.